First published in the UK in 2016 by
Connie Stokes Publishing

www.conniestokespublishing.co.uk

Copyright text © Rachel Hayward 2015
Copyright illustration © Bill Greenhead 2015

ISBN 978-0-9935927-0-6

To Jack,

Happy Reading!

Rachel Hayward

For my three favourite boys,
Olliebear, Will and Eddie

Secret Agent Oliver
and the
Football Foe Fighters

Written by Rachel Hayward
Illustrated by Bill Greenhead

Contents

Prologue

Now You See Me, Now You Don't

'This way please, this way. Keep close together now.' Tom Plank, part time tour guide for Southdale United, was leading a tour of excited supporters through the back corridors of Duke Park Stadium. He stopped at a set of double doors.

'Right, one, two, three… eleven, twelve. Great, all here. Now we are about to enter a very secure area and there are a few rules. No cameras, no disturbing the players or management team and that includes no asking for autographs. Please can everyone keep together in a line on the left hand side.' Tom began to open the door.

'WOW!' a little boy yelled. 'It's like entering the Bat Cave.'

The tour group obediently followed Tom until they reached the players' tunnel. Their eyes were wide open as they watched the activity.

Tom began to count the line again. 'Eleven, twelve, thirteen. Thirteen?' He looked over his list. That can't be right, he thought as he checked his clipboard. 'Yes, twelve it says.' He counted again and sure enough there were thirteen. 'Right everyone, if I call your name out, please come and stand to my right.' As he did the roll call again, all the supporters obediently shuffled themselves over to his right. Once he was finished he looked up. There was no one left so he turned and counted again. This time he counted only twelve. Confused, he rubbed his eyes.

That was close, Roger Bunney, mad scientist and illusionist extraordinaire, thought after he had made himself invisible again.

'Should have gone to spec...hey, there's Kevin Carter,' cried the little boy from earlier.

The crowd began to ooh and ah as Southdale United's star striker sauntered past them with an air of arrogance and made his way to the pitch. Tom quickly ushered the tour party to their seats and the game kicked off.

Woah! The crowd went wild as Kevin scored his 100th goal for the team. He ran to the corner of the pitch to celebrate. They chanted his name as he cupped his hands around his ears to egg them on.

A second later, the whistle was blown and the teams made their way into the tunnel for half time. Supporters, stretching over the railing, greeted them with cheers.

'Carter, Carter…' one man shouted. It was Roger Bunney. 'Please can you sign my programme?'

Kevin shrugged the man away. He wasn't going to sign another thing until the club agreed to a pay rise. After all, Kevin had pulled the team through victory after victory. They wouldn't have been top of the table without him. They owed him, he thought as he pushed open the door to the Manager's room to demand it.

'Not a chance are you getting a pay rise,' the manager, Miguel Le Verve, said so loudly he could be heard from the hall.

'You'll regret this,' Kevin growled as he burst out of the room slamming the door into the steward's nose.

'Watch it!' Kevin yelled.

'You opened the door on me,' grumbled the steward, Benjamin Bunney.

'Shouldn't have been spying then, should you?'

'Ignore my oaf of a cousin, Carter. He's always walking into doors.' Kevin and Benjamin spun around to see the strange little man holding out a programme and pen.

'He's your cousin?' Kevin asked as he looked over the two polar opposites.

'Yes, unfortunately. Before you go, please can you sign my programme? You're my hero.'

Begrudgingly, Kevin grabbed the pen and scribbled.

'Erm..could you write it 'to my super fan, Roger Bunney'?'

When he was finished, Kevin shoved the programme back to Roger and stormed out.

'To my super fan,' Benjamin mocked. 'What are you doing here anyway? You weren't on the tour.'

'Are you sure about that?'

'Are you using that awful hocus pocus again?'

'It's not hocus pocus. It's illusion.'

'What kind of job is that anyway?'

'The best kind. I make people believe in magic.'

Suddenly they were interrupted by shouting from the stands. Only a matter of seconds into the second half and a huge fight had broken out on the pitch with Kevin Carter right in the middle. When his team-mates finally managed to prise him away, the referee held up a red card. This seemed to anger Kevin even more and his team-mates had to drag him off the pitch kicking and screaming.

'We won't condone such bad behaviour,' the manager said to him after the game.

'Phah!' Kevin shouted, kicking his energy drink across the changing room and hitting one of the other players on the head.

'I have no choice but to kick you off the team.'

'You can't do that,' Kevin hissed. 'I'm your best player.'

'That's no longer enough,' the manager said nodding to Benjamin Bunney.

'Yes boss,' Benjamin said as he grabbed Kevin and turfed him out onto the street.

'You can't do this. I have nowhere else to go.' Benjamin closed the door in Kevin's face. 'I'll get you back for this,' Kevin shouted before he sank down to the kerb.

'Kevin Carter, my hero?'

Kevin looked up to see the odd little man, Roger Bunney again, peering over him. 'What do you want?'

Roger Bunney grinned.

Chapter 1

Mission Control

'Watch it kid,' a grumpy voice yelled. Oliver, running excitedly into the Southdale United store, had bumped into a man whose collar was pulled up around his cheeks and whose cap cast a shadow over his face.

'Sorry,' Oliver said. For a second Oliver thought he recognised him but the man scuttled off down the street muttering before he could catch a good look at his face.

'Silly kids, silly fans, silly kids who are fans. They're the worst,' the man grumbled as he lifted his collar even more.

'Well! You look like a boy on a mission,' the shop keeper said to Oliver.

'I am. I am here to buy a new game for my console.'

'Are you now?'

'Yes, with my birthday vouchers.'

'Is it your birthday?' he asked.

'Yes, 8 today.'

'Well I think an 8 year old birthday boy deserves some special treatment. Don't you? I'm going to take you to our VIP till.'

Oliver grabbed a copy of the game he wanted and followed the shop keeper to the till. He was intrigued.

'A special cashier for a special birthday boy,' the shop keeper said before he walked away.

Oliver's gaze turned to the counter. The cashier was none other than the Southdale United captain, Simon Walker. 'Wow! What are you doing here?' Oliver asked.

'It's a special charity day today,' Walker said. 'For one day only, I will be serving all of our lovely supporters. And what is it you are buying?'

'A game for my console.'

'Well, I'll tell you what. If you promise to be me the first time you play, I'll sign your copy.'

'Ah, mega!' Oliver said.

'So who am I signing it for?'

'My name is Oliver.'

'OK. Dear Oliver,' he said as he wrote. 'I hope you're the winner.'

Oliver, with his surfer style haircut and steely green eyes, couldn't keep the smile off his face. He smiled all the way home and all the way through dinner and bath time until he finally got to pop the game in the console and start to play. He sat on the end of his bed playing all evening until finally, he completed the last level. Before he knew it, a voice boomed from the TV screen accompanied by some celebratory music and fireworks exploding across the screen. 'You are the winner!' it said. He had only been playing for two hours and he had already managed to complete all 6 levels. Maybe it was because he had been the invincible Simon Walker, he thought.

Oliver put down the control and jumped to his feet. He started dancing around the room to the sound of the music like no-one was looking and no-one was. Or so he thought. 'I'm a winner, I'm a winner,' he sang to himself.

All of a sudden, the music stopped and a man appeared on the screen. Oliver stopped dancing and listened.

'My name is Michael Hancock and I am Southdale United's Safety Officer. Congratulations on completing the final level. You are one of a small number of people clever enough to do this. That's why we, Southdale United, need you,' he said as his finger reached out of the TV and seemed to almost touch Oliver's nose.

Oliver jumped back but the man continued. 'We need you to type this code into our website and you will get your mission.'

A number appeared on the screen and Oliver quickly scrambled around until he found a pen and paper. He just managed to scribble down the number when the game powered down.

'Oliver, bed time,' his mum called.

'But mum...'

'No arguments. It's late.'

'Oh!' He would just have to wait to continue his adventure.

The following morning, remembering the events of the night before, Oliver leapt out of bed and ran over to his computer. Logging onto Southdale United's website he entered the code. Moments later, the computer seemed to shut down. Oh no, he thought. It was a virus. He was just about to unplug it when Michael Hancock appeared on the screen.

'I'm glad you made it. I am on the hunt for a team of clever individuals to be our intelligence outside the Club. Select your team wisely because this work is confidential and very important. Do you accept this position?'

Oliver nodded at the screen unable to speak.

'Good. When the time is right, you will hear from me again. Until then, study everything.' With that Michael stood up and saluted.

Chapter 2

The Vanishing Team

Lying on his Southdale United bedspread, Oliver watched the highlights of last weekend's game. Not a single incident to report. Oliver was secretly disappointed. It had been ages since Michael Hancock spoke to him from inside the computer and the only communication since then had been a brief report on a series of threatening letters to the club written by someone claiming to be The Mysterious Shadow.

Just then he leapt forward, squinting. Could it have been...? He pressed rewind and moved closer. One, two…pause.

'YES,' he yelled. Inside the service tunnel was a mysterious figure, his face hidden by shadows.

That must be him, Oliver thought.

That second, a letter popped under his bedroom door. He was full of excitement as he jumped off the bed and snatched it up. The envelope read: Secret Agent Oliver, Football Foe Fighters HQ, Bedroom in the Attic, 23 Bandsrook Road, Southdale. His hands trembled as he ripped it open.

Southdale United

Dear Secret Agent Oliver,

It has recently come to our attention that The Mysterious Shadow has started his attacks. We call on you to help us before it is too late.

Yours
Michael Hancock
Safety Officer
Southdale United

Oliver ran to his desk and picked up his radio. **'Alert! Alert!** Calling all users. Please report to Headquarters with immediate effect.'

No sooner had he put the radio down when there was a knocking on the door. Oliver opened it up to his cousins, Will and Eddie.

'Where do you want us, boss?' Will, the oldest and cleverest of the group at 13, asked.

'What's happened?' Eddie could not hide the thrill in his voice. Eddie was 10 and really sporty so working for his favourite football club was like a dream come true.

'Positions, team. We're on.'

Without hesitation the team bustled into the room and started to work in their assigned positions.

Later that week Oliver and Eddie took to their seats in the Duke Park Stadium, a great position to watch the crowd.

'What're we looking for?' asked Eddie.

'Keep your eyes peeled for unusual activity,' Oliver replied.

'How's the camera looking, Will?' Eddie asked quietly into his button hole. He had a camera hooked up to the collar of his coat so that they had sight of everything.

'It needs adjusting slightly upwards,' Will said through the radio from HQ.

Eddie followed instructions. 'Is that better?'

'Perfect,' replied Will.

The game kicked off and the Football Foe Fighters, as they had named themselves, watched on. Will was keeping a close eye on the pitch and players' tunnel from the television screen in HQ. Meanwhile, Oliver and Eddie paid close attention to the crowd around them.

'HQ to boss.'

'Go ahead HQ.'

'On the pitch. Kyle Turner has just…well he has disappeared,' William said in bewilderment.

'What do you mean, disappeared?' Oliver asked.

'One minute he was there, on the half way line and the next…well he wasn't. Maybe it's the TV screen,' he said, trying to find a rational explanation.

But he was right, Oliver realised. Southdale United were down to 10 men. The man in the seat next to Oliver rubbed his eyes and said, 'Did you see that too? Where did he go?'

'Michael Parks has gone too,' said Eddie.

'Right, over to you, Will,' Oliver said.

Back at HQ, Will looked over the recordings.

'Quickly, Will,' said Oliver. Jerome Lavigne and Simon Walker had now vanished.

'It's the ball,' Will shouted. 'Every time anyone kicks it they vanish.'

'Great work. Right Eddie, let's go,' Oliver ordered.

'What's the plan?' Eddie asked as they ran down the players' tunnel.

'The saboteur, AKA, The Mysterious Shadow wants to ruin Southdale's chance at winning anything,' said Will, 'so I reckon if we get the players back in time to win the game we'll have beaten him.'

'I think you're right, Will,' said Oliver.

'Look,' shouted Eddie pointing to a ball at the edge of the pitch. 'That looks like the official ball.'

'The saboteur must have switched it,' Oliver said.

'What are you going to do?' Eddie asked as Oliver picked it up.

'I think I need to follow the players. Maybe if I get them to kick the real ball it will bring them back. At least it's worth a try,' Oliver said as he burst through the stewards' line and onto the pitch. Running as fast as possible towards the ball, before the referee could stop him, he lifted his leg and swung it forward with all of his might.

As quick as a blink, Oliver found himself on the moon's surface wearing a rather large space suit. 'Wow,' he said to himself. 'I wasn't expecting that.'

His eyes panned the vast and empty space until he saw Kyle Turner prancing around. He seemed to be enjoying the lightness of his body as he bounced up and down over the craters.

'Kyle, Kyle. I've come to save you.'

'Why? It's fun up here,' Kyle said.

'Aren't you scared?'

'Well, I was at first but then I realised how much fun it was.' He started to bounce again.

'If I don't get you back before the end Southdale United may lose the game.'

That startled the striker and he obediently followed Oliver's lead. Oliver grabbed hold of

Kyle's hand, placed the ball on the floor and told him to kick it. The next moment, they were back on the pitch, the crowd cheering loudly from the stands.

'I must save the others,' Oliver told Kyle. 'Don't let anyone but me kick that ball,' he said pointing to the fake ball.

A few seconds later Oliver kicked the ball again and landed in the middle of a bush. A piercing, screeching noise filled his ears. He poked his head out, expecting to see a large bird of prey, but instead saw Michael Parks running frantically through the woodland, screaming like a baby. It wasn't long before Oliver saw why he was so frightened. Parks was being chased by a Tyrannosaurus with a vicious-looking face.

Oliver launched himself out of the bush ahead of

the oncoming defender. Soon they were running alongside one another.

'I've come to take you home,' he puffed.

'Well hurry up, please hurry up!'

'Kick the ball,' Oliver shouted, as he threw it in front of them and grabbed Michael's hand.

The confused defender looked from the ball to the dinosaur. 'What the heck, it's not like I have many choices,' he said as he kicked the ball into the sky.

Having returned Michael Parks safely to the stadium, Oliver noticed that there were only nine minutes left to save Jerome Lavigne and Simon Walker. He kicked the ball into the corner of the net.

Before he knew it, Oliver had landed on sand, and he spun around to take in his surroundings. He was in the middle of an empty desert.

Then something caught his eye - a sandcastle. As he got closer, he noticed something lumpy in the sand next to it. Using his hands, he began to dig. His hand touched a man's foot and he heard a giggle.

'Stop, I'm ticklish.' Lavigne had covered his body in sand, his head poking out of the top.

'Jerome, I have come to save you.'

'I could have done with you when the camel was trying to get me. I had to hide in the sand to make him go away. How did I get here anyway?'

Oliver, no time to explain, grabbed Jerome's hand and soon they were back on the pitch.

'Back of the net.' Oliver began to celebrate his penalty scoring ability when suddenly...Splash! He had landed in the ocean. He spotted Simon Walker struggling at a reef wearing an old-fashioned, round diving mask. Oliver touched his own mask. That's how I can breathe, he thought.

Walker's foot was caught in the reef. Oliver reached down and tried to pull it out but his shoe-lace was all tangled up. Then a little family of turtles arrived and began to nibble away at it. It soon became free and Walker gestured thank you to the turtles with a bow. They bowed back and swam away.

'Quick,' Oliver mouthed, 'no time.' He pointed to his watch and then dropped the ball which slowly sank down onto the sea bed.

'Kick it,' he mimed, grabbing Walker's hand.

'Oh, no, no, no, no...,' cried Roger Bunney as he watched from the stands as Oliver and team captain, Simon Walker, appeared back on the pitch. 'How did he figure it out? Kevin will be furious.' He scurried up the stairway to the concourse and out of the turnstiles as quickly as he could.

ROAR! Duke Park Stadium was bouncing as the crowd jumped up and down celebrating the goal that Simon Walker had just scored with only four seconds left on the clock. He turned and winked at Oliver.

'Good work Football Foe Fighters,' Oliver said through the radio.

Chapter 3

Time for a Dance?

'Ha-ha-ha-ha,' Kevin Carter's cackle echoed off the walls. 'They will not be able to stop me this time,' he said as he poured potions together in the locked kitroom. With the help of mad scientist and illusionist Roger Bunney, his new plan would surely ruin the team's chances, forever. That will teach them, he thought.

Not long after Kevin's demise, he had managed to convince everyone that he was a changed man just enough to land the job as kitman from where he had ample opportunity to destroy Southdale United.

There was a knock on the door and someone tried

the handle. Kevin quickly rushed around the room hiding all the bottles, or so he thought.

'What are you doing in there?' the manager, Miguel Le Verve, said when the door opened.

'I'm just washing the kit, sir,' Kevin said in a soft voice. 'The lock must be faulty.'

'Well, I wanted to make sure you got my change to the team selection.'

'Yes, sir, and the kits are almost ready.'

'Good. Ooh, soda. I'm quite thirsty today,' Le Verve said as he reached out and picked up a bottle from the side.

'NO!' Kevin shouted.

Miguel Le Verve was quite shocked. He hadn't heard Kevin shout that loud since his old playing days.

'I only have enough for the players, sir,' Kevin said taking the bottle from him. 'I have put plenty of water in your lounge.'

'Very well.'

After Le Verve had left, Kevin closed the door and slunk back against it. 'Phew, that was close.' He bent down and peered into the shadows where Roger Bunney was hiding. 'You'd better start clearing this lot away while I set the trap,' he said scooping up the soda bottles.

'I'd say it was good to see you Secret Agent Oliver,' said Michael, Southdale United's Safety Officer, as he shook Oliver's hand and walked him and Eddie through the main entrance, 'but that means The Mysterious Shadow is back.'

'Indeed,' said Oliver.

'Great work with that magic ball. That was a close call. Any idea what he has planned next?'

'Not yet, but I'm confident we'll stop him.'

'I hope so.'

'You can count on the Football Foe Fighters,' Eddie said.

'Right, Eddie, let's go pitch side. HQ, keep an eye out for unusual activity,' Oliver instructed through his button-hole microphone. Will was holding the fort back at HQ.

Nothing at all had happened in the first half. No mischief or mayhem. In fact, not even a goal. Oliver sat back in one of the photographer's chairs and yawned. Half-time was just finishing and the players made their way back onto the pitch.

'HQ to boss.'

'Go ahead, HQ. What have you got?'

'It's Rory Webster,' Will said. 'It looks like he's got ants in his pants.' Eddie and Oliver turned their gaze to Rory, who was wiggling his hips like a crazy.

'Do you think he needs a wee?' said Eddie.

Rory Webster was shaking his bottom so fast that vibrations started to ripple through the pitch.

'No, it looks like he's…dancing,' Oliver corrected.

'Look at Kristov Vianchigo,' Will shouted suddenly. 'Is that the Flamenco he's dancing?'

Seconds later, star striker, Sylvester Bernard, threw himself to the floor and was spinning around on his back with his legs in the air. 'Right team, let's go,' said Oliver.

As they ran down to the touchline, goalkeeper Sam Grimshaw, who had veered so far away from the goal that even the lousiest of strikers would be able to score, was jiving his way straight towards Oliver. Luckily, the other team was so distracted by the dancing that no-one took a shot at the empty goal.

'Sorry,' Grimshaw said as he bumped into Oliver, nearly sending him flying. 'I just can't seem to stop myself.'

'Tell me, Sam, did anything unusual happen at half time?'

'No, I don't think so, just the usual pep talk and refreshments.'

When they reached the dressing room, Eddie was panting and reached out for a fizzy purple energy drink that had been left on the side. 'Perfect, I'm so thirsty after that run.'

'No,' shouted Oliver. 'Don't drink it. Sam Grimshaw said something about refreshments.'

But it was too late. Eddie had already gulped down half of the purple liquid and had started to do the Robot right in front of Oliver.

'It's definitely something in the drink that's making them all dance, boss,' Will said. 'You'll need to try and find an antidote.'

'Great idea, Will.'

Oliver hurried off down the corridor to find some kind of antidote leaving Eddie to robo-dance himself all the way back to the pitch where Will could keep an eye on him through the CCTV.

Kevin the kitman gasped as he spotted Oliver letting himself into the kitroom. He was about to follow after him but stopped in his tracks. 'Too obvious,' Kevin thought. The last thing he wanted was for the Football Foe Fighters to discover he was behind the madness. He had to think of another way, and quickly. Spotting the stewards' phone, he ran over and called Event Control.

Oliver, searching through the cupboards, soon found a strange bottle hidden under the sink. It was the same purple colour as the drinks, and the label read 'Dancing Antidote'.

'Too easy,' he shouted down the radio. 'I have found the antidote.'

'Really,' said Will. 'Where was it?'

'In the kitroom.'

'You have to be quick. Only five minutes left on the clock,' Will told him.

'Quick,' Kevin called as he dashed towards the closed door followed closely by the steward, Benjamin Bunney. 'Someone has broken into the kitroom.'

They barged through the door to find an empty room.

'We're too late,' said Bunney.

'That's because you were too slow, you big oaf!' Roger shouted as he magically appeared.

'Hey, what are you doing here?' Benjamin asked.

'Watching you be a complete buffoon.'

'Who's the buffoon?' Kevin whispered sharply in Roger's ears. 'I told you to clear everything away.'

'But I did,' said Roger.

'You left the antidote.'

Roger blushed as Kevin dashed out of the room and towards the pitch.

By the time Oliver arrived at the touchline, all the players had started to dance a cancan around the stadium. Stewards and supporters, who weren't sure what was going on, had been forced to join in.

Oliver threw the antidote to Sam Grimshaw. 'Drink some and pass it on,' he called out.

One slurp was enough and the dancing stopped.

'We did it,' Will cheered.

'Yes, another good job, team,' Oliver said. 'But

it's not over yet. We need to find out who is doing this.'

'Arghhhh...' shouted Kevin as he watched his most recent plan to scupper the game fizzle out. 'I'll out-smart you soon, Football Foe Fighters.'

With that Kevin and Roger disappeared back into the shadows.

Chapter 4

Football Frenzy

Football Foe Fighters HQ was a hive of activity. Eddie and Will were watching replays of the recent games on their computers trying to find evidence. Oliver was busy setting up a whiteboard in front of the window.

'Right, team, huddle around. Let's take a look at the clues.'

'Well boss,' Will said, 'the saboteur must have had access to the ball and the energy drinks, so I'd say he works there and the antidote was found in the kitroom so it could be the kitman.'

'Isn't that a bit obvious?' Eddie asked.

'Eddie's right. Let's not make assumptions too soon.'

'He could work for The FA,' said Eddie.

'Or he could be one of the ball boys,' Will added.

'Okay. Let's make a list of all the possible groups. Will, I want you to cross check against the staff list. Let's narrow it down.' He looked at his watch. 'Eddie and I had better head down to Duke Park Stadium.'

It was the last game in April and the spring sun was beating down on the stands. Music started to pound through the speakers.

'What have you got for us, Will?' Oliver asked through his radio.

'I've narrowed it down to three main groups, boss: the match officials, the backroom staff and the management team.'

'Southdale United's backroom staff and management?' Eddie asked.

'Yes. At no point did the opposition have access to our team's drinks.'

'Great. Will, can you watch the Match Officials through the CCTV? Eddie, I want you to watch the Management team and I will keep an eye on the backroom staff.'

'Ha-ha-ha. They will never catch me from here,' said Kevin, sitting in one of the men's toilets.

'You okay in there?' A voice called making him jump. It was a steward on his rounds.

'Fine,' Kevin snapped.

'You're going to miss the start of the game.'

'Can't be helped.' Kevin started to blow raspberries from his mouth.

'Eww,' the steward said. 'I'll leave you to it.' And he rushed out of the toilets.

'I won't miss the game,' Kevin said to himself switching on a mini television that was on his knee.

The Football Foe Fighters' favourite team were on a roll. Only five minutes left until injury time and they were five goals up. Sylvester Bernard had scored a hat-trick whilst Kyle Turner and Pete Dunne had scored one each.

'What a game!' Will said down the radio.

'I know,' Oliver said thoughtfully.

'What's the matter?'

'Well, surprisingly, nothing bad has happened yet.'

'That's a good thing isn't it?'

'Mmm,' Oliver replied.

'Oh, no,' Eddie said dancing around wildly at the side of the pitch where the ball boys were crouching.

'What's wrong?' asked Will, watching him on CCTV. 'Have you drunk the dancing juice again?'

'No,' Eddie said. 'I need the toilet.'

'Oh,' Oliver and Will called down the radio in unison. 'Be quick.'

'I don't like it. Something is not right. Why has he not done anything yet?' Oliver said.

'Maybe he's not here. He could be sick,' said Will. 'I'll get a list of staff that haven't shown up.'

'I'm not sure that's necessary,' radioed Oliver.

Kyle Turner had just taken a strike at goal when the ball, inches away from the goal line, spun back around like a boomerang and hit the celebrating striker on the bottom, knocking him to the ground. The ball then shot down the pitch like a rocket, right into Southdale United's goal. The away team supporters jumped up and down, cheering.

'Own goal by Kyle Turner - or our saboteur?' Oliver mumbled to himself. 'Will, anything to report?'

'Nothing. The match officials look as confused as anyone. What about you?'

'Same here. Most of the backroom staff are just sitting watching the game. There are a couple of people missing, though.'

The ball was now whizzing around, knocking Southdale United players to the ground and bouncing in and out of the opposition's goal. The score was now 5-4. Sam Grimshaw had never looked so frazzled as he jumped up and down, left and right, trying his best to stop the ball getting in the back of the net.

Eddie ran into the toilets as quickly as he could. He always left going to the toilet to the last minute.

Kevin the kitman peered under the door and watched the Football Foe Fighter run into the cubicle next door. Oh no, I need to get out of here, he thought. Quietly, he unlocked his door and made a dash for the exit.

When Eddie was finished he came out to find the door to the next cubicle swinging back and forth. Wondering why, he took a step closer and saw a mini TV and something else on the floor.

'Eddie to Oliver,' he shouted through the radio.

'What is it Eddie?' Oliver asked.

'You will never guess what I've found.'

Oliver ran quickly to the top of the tunnel to meet Eddie.

'What is it, Eddie?' Will asked.

'It's a remote control.'

'It must have been used to control the ball,' Oliver said. 'How do we use it?'

Will brought the instructions up on his computer and talked them through it. Within seconds they had control of the ball again and landed it safely back on the centre spot just as the referee blew his whistle.

'Phew, that was close,' said Eddie.

'Yes it was,' said Oliver. 'I never thought I'd say this, Eddie, but I am glad that you leave going to the toilet to the last minute.'

The team laughed.

Chapter 5

Monkey Mayhem

Secret Agent Oliver sat on a bench outside Duke Park Stadium. He was watching the crowd mill around the fan zone as he waited for his team, the Football Foe Fighters, to return with their lunch. He was deep in thought, as Eddie tapped him on the shoulder making him jump.

'What's the matter?' Eddie asked.

'I don't like being stumped,' Oliver replied. He scratched his head and thought back to the last few games: a magic transporting ball, a dancing drink and a remote-controlled ball. Whatever next?

'We're going to catch him, boss. We are the

Football Foe Fighters. We can do anything,' said Will reassuringly.

'You're right, Will. We need to stay positive. Right, team, gather around.' He pulled out his tablet and opened a folder marked Shortlisted Suspects. 'So what do we know?' he asked.

'Well, we know that whoever it is has been here for the last three games,' said Eddie.

'Yes, and that means that it can't be the match officials as they have been different each game,' added Will.

'We also know that it can't be the ball boys,' said Eddie, 'as they were on the pitch when the ball was being controlled from the toilets.'

'So we have narrowed it down to three suspects who were out of sight at the last game and who had access to the kitroom,' said Oliver as he clicked on the first of three photos.

'Benjamin Bunney,' Will said. 'He is the tunnel steward. He's always there.'

'But he is a bit dopey,' added Eddie.

'How about you keep an eye on him, Will?'

'No problem, boss,' Will said.

Next up was Tom Plank. Tom was the Pitchside Tour Guide.

'He is never around when the ball is in play,' said Eddie.

'Okay, so I want you to find out what he is doing.'

'Will do,' Eddie said.

'Finally we have Kevin Carter.'

'THE Kevin Carter?' Eddie asked.

'The one and only.'

'Kevin is only the best striker that played for Southdale United,' Eddie explained excitedly.

'And the angriest,' said Oliver.

'Not any more boss,' continued Eddie. 'He's a reformed character since his new role as kitman.'

'Don't judge a book by its cover,' warned Oliver. 'I'll watch him.'

'I've logged into the CCTV system on my tablet,'

said Will, 'so remember, any unusual activity, radio it through and I'll zoom in to check it out.'

'Good luck, team,' Oliver said finally. 'Let's go.'

The penultimate game of the season kicked off. The Football Foe Fighters were in position and ready. After only a few moments, the crowd at Duke Park Stadium were going wild as Sylvester Bernard scored the first goal of the game within less than a minute.

'I think it is going to be a good game,' Eddie said.

'I think you're right,' replied Oliver, 'but let's keep focused on the job in hand, team.'

'Will to Oliver,' Will called through the radio.

'Go ahead, Will,' Oliver answered.

'Benjamin Bunney is on the move.'

'What's he doing?' Oliver asked.

Will followed Benjamin out of the players' tunnel and onto the concourse.

'It looks like he's…buying chips,' Will groaned, a little disappointed that it wasn't something a bit more sinister. 'I don't think he's our guy, boss.'

'Eddie, any news on Tom Plank?' Oliver asked.

'Not really. I followed him into the lounge but he is just sitting at a table with some of the staff drinking a cup of tea,' Eddie replied.

The crowd in the stands began to roar again as

the ball flew into the away goal. Southdale United players were celebrating at the side of the pitch.

'Who scored?' asked Eddie.

'I don't know, I was too busy watching Kev… Woah,' yelled Oliver. 'Where's he going?'

Kevin the kitman was running as fast as he could down the side of the pitch. The Football Foe Fighters set off after him.

'What's that he's running towards?' Eddie asked, panting.

'It looks like a cage,' Oliver replied.

'And it's filled with monkeys,' Will said.

'Oh no, we've got to stop him,' Oliver shouted, picking up speed.

But it was too late. Kevin the kitman had released the lock and suddenly dozens of monkeys were running out onto the pitch. They picked up the ball and started to play piggy-in-the-middle with some confused players.

'Hey, give us the ball back,' the team captain, Simon Walker, called out. He hadn't noticed that one cheeky monkey had tied his shoelaces together. 'Woah,' he yelled as he tripped over his own feet.

'Ha-ha-ha,' Kevin the kitman cackled as he watched the chaos. I'd better get out of here, he thought, as Oliver and Eddie approached.

'Shall we go after him?' Eddie asked.

'There's no time, we need to catch the monkeys,' Oliver told him. 'Will, you follow him. It looks as though he is heading for the service tunnel.'

'Sure thing, boss,'

'Football Foe Fighters to the rescue,' Eddie called out as he and Oliver chased after the naughty little monkeys.

Sam Grimshaw didn't know what was going on when three of the monkeys began swinging around in his goal. 'Shoo, shoo,' he said trying to usher them out. Before he knew it, one of them had run behind him and pulled down his shorts. The crowd roared with laughter at such a sight.

'Oi,' he shouted, 'that's not fair.'

Oliver and Eddie had finally managed to round up all the monkeys. Well almost all.

'There's a baby one left over there,' Oliver pointed out. 'Quick, catch him.'

The cheeky little monkey was eating a banana in the centre circle, when he saw the pair closing in. He threw the banana skin behind him and scuttled off across the pitch. Eddie didn't have time to stop as the banana skin landed on the floor right in front of him.

'Help,' he yelled as his foot slipped on the skin which sent him skidding all the way down the pitch until…Bump! He crash-landed right on top of the last monkey. The crowd cheered.

'Well done Eddie, you did it. Will, do you have an update on Kevin Carter?' Oliver asked through his radio.

'Sorry boss. I followed him all the way out of the ground and watched him jump onto a bus towards town.'

'Don't worry. Now that we know who the saboteur is, we'll get him for sure next time.'

Chapter 6

The Final Storm

'Are you certain it's him?' Michael, the Safety Officer, asked as they walked towards the steward's meeting.

'Never been more certain of anything,' Oliver told him. Secret Agent Oliver was explaining how he and his team had managed to piece the clues together until they finally found out who the The Mysterious Shadow was.

'Well I never. What on earth could push a man to behave like that?'

'Pride,' Oliver explained. 'Kevin was flying high as Southdale United's star striker. In many people's eyes, the team was only in the league because of him. When he got booted out, pardon the pun, his pride was hurt.'

'But that was ages ago.'

'Some wounds never heal.'

'That's not all though. We think he has been having help.'

'From who?'

'I don't know but there is no way he could have learnt how to make a magic ball or dancing juice on his own.'

'I see,' the Safety Officer said as they came to a halt. They had reached their destination. The other Football Foe Fighters were already there, armed with piles of photos that they were handing out.

'This is Kevin Carter,' the Safety Officer began, holding up a copy of the picture for all to see. 'AKA a Southdale United legend, AKA our kitman, AKA the saboteur, AKA The Mysterious Shadow.'

The group gasped. 'You are kidding?' someone called out.

'It can't be,' said another.

'I'm afraid so,' Oliver confirmed, 'and we are pretty sure he has an accomplice.'

'Someone who knows a little about potions,' said Will.

'Or magic,' continued Eddie.

Benjamin Bunney's eyes widened and he

nervously stepped backwards into the crowd of stewards.

'As you all know,' the Safety Officer went on, 'today is the last game of the season and a win will secure the title for us. Needless to say, tensions will be running high.'

'I have no doubt that the saboteur will strike again, only this time will be different,' Oliver chimed in, 'because he knows we are on to him so he will try and blend into the crowd.'

'I want everybody to be extra vigilant today,' the Safety Officer said. 'Report anything unusual.'

As soon as the briefing was over Benjamin Bunney quickly made his way to a quiet corner. He pulled out his mobile and made a call to his cousin, Roger.

'It's you, isn't it?' he asked as soon as Roger had picked up.

'What is?'

'You're working with Kevin Carter. Together you are The Mysterious Shadow.'

'Keep your voice down,' Roger hissed. 'Someone might hear you.'

'So what? Maybe I should tell them. I always thought your friendship with him was odd.'

'Wait, wait. You're right,' said Roger. 'It was wrong. I'll turn myself in. Will you meet me first?'

'Fine but this is your only chance. Either you turn yourself in or I will.'

The sun was beating down on the stands. There was another heat wave and it was all Oliver could do to stop himself stripping off to keep cool. There were stewards walking up and down the stands handing out free water.

'Make sure you keep drinking,' Oliver told the team as he grabbed a couple of bottles. 'We can't afford for anyone to get too thirsty today.'

'Will to Michael,' Will called through the radio.

'Go ahead, Will.' Michael answered from his position in Event Control.

'Any sightings?'

'No, none yet.'

'Boss,' Eddie said.

'Yes?'

'What if he doesn't return today?'

'He will, Eddie, he will.'

At that very moment a cloud passed over the stadium.

'What!' Will called out.

Their mouths fell open and the crowd gasped as they watched snowflakes fall from the sky. 'I've never heard of it snowing at the end of May,' Eddie said.

'Michael,' Oliver called, 'any idea what's going on?'

'No. There is no mention of a snow shower on the weather report.'

'I'd say this is more than a shower,' said Eddie.

'I'd say you werc right,' said Oliver.

The blizzard was now so thick that they could barely see the pitch. Will pulled out a telescope from his pocket, extended it and handed it to Oliver.

'This should help,' he said.

'Great.' Oliver looked through the telescope and altered the focus until he could see better. The referee had blown his whistle and was waving his arms around calling the game to a halt. The players seemed more than happy with this decision as they were freezing in their shorts and T-shirts.

Both teams made a dash for the tunnel but the snow had already started to settle and the ground was now too slippery for them to run on. Simon Walker lost his footing and went skidding down the side of the pitch, taking out Kyle Turner and Michael Parks as he went.

'Ah, watch out!' yelled Rory Webster as he quickly followed in Simon Walker's path. Before they knew it all four players had landed in a heap at the mouth of the tunnel.

'We need to do something, team, and quickly,' said Oliver.

'But what can we do about the weather?' asked Eddie.

'This is not down to the weather,' Oliver said. 'I suspect foul play.'

'Kevin the kitman Carter?' Will yelled in disbelief.

'The one and only.'

'This is your doing, isn't it?' Benjamin said as he met with Roger.

'What are you talking about, you big oaf? Even I'm not clever enough to control the weather,' he lied. 'Right, I'm ready to turn myself in.'

Benjamin started to follow him when suddenly Roger disappeared. 'Hey, where are you?' he shouted as he spun around looking for his cousin. He hadn't noticed that Roger had tied a rope to his belt clip and each time the steward spun around he became more and more tangled up. When he couldn't budge anymore, Roger reappeared and tied the knot even tighter.

'You big oaf. You really think I would turn myself in and go to prison?' He leant forward. 'Look into my eyes, look into my eyes,' he said, hypnotising his cousin. 'When you wake, you are going to forget all about my involvement and have no recollection of who tied you up.' Then he made himself invisible and clicked his fingers.

By the time the Football Foe Fighters got down to the pitch, the grounds team were out in their winter coats desperately trying to shovel the snow off the pitch but they couldn't clear it as quick as it was falling.

'How do you think he is doing it, boss?' asked Will.

'I don't know. Michael, anything your end?'

'No, but the radios are going berserk from the stewards calling in unusual activity.'

'Look,' shouted Will, 'up there.' He pointed to the sky. It was hard for them to see with snowflakes falling into their eyes but they could just about make out the shape of a helicopter.

'That's it,' shouted Eddie. 'A snow cannon on a helicopter.'

'I need to get up there,' Oliver said.

'I know where the stairs to the roof are,' Will said. 'Follow me.'

The team made it to the roof but the helicopter was still too far away.

'What are you going to do now?' Will asked.

'Here,' Eddie called out. He had found a rope and

was tying a loop into it. 'Everybody grab a section.'

They did as they were told and, before they knew it, they had whipped it into a lasso above their heads.

'Ready, one, two, three…' The loop flew into the air and hooked itself onto the foot of the helicopter.

'Good work team. Now hold tight, I'm going up.' Oliver began to climb.

'Oh no!' Kevin the kitman yelled as the helicopter tipped to one side and Secret Agent Oliver appeared at the open doorway. 'What are you doing here?'

'I've come to stop you,' Oliver told him.

'Ha-ha-ha! Stop me? You are not clever enough to stop me!'

'Want to bet on that?' Oliver leapt forward and pushed Kevin off his seat.

As the pair started to roll about on the floor of the unpiloted helicopter, Oliver snuck out an elastic band from his pocket. Before Kevin even knew what was going on, Oliver had tied his hands together around the leg of the chair. Quickly, Oliver jumped to his feet and took hold of the joystick.

He was just in time as the helicopter was about to crash straight into one of the lounges. There were crowds of people at the window, horrified. Oliver managed to veer the helicopter around and finally

landed it on the centre circle where his team, the Safety Officer and several police officers were waiting.

'And the award for cleverness and bravery goes to….The Football Foe Fighters.'

The crowd cheered as Oliver and his team took to the stage.

It was later that evening and following Southdale United's great win, the owners had invited all the staff to a celebratory party for winning the league and for finally capturing the saboteur.

'We did it, boss,' Will whispered into his ear on the stage.

'We would have done it a lot sooner if we'd have listened to you at the start,' Oliver said.

'You were right not to assume too early. We had to be certain.'

'Well it's not quite over yet,' Oliver frowned.

'His accomplice is still out there.'

'Not for long,' Will said.

'Not with the Football Foe Fighters around,' finished Eddie.

With that they lifted their awards in the air and the crowd cheered.

The End

SOUTHDALE UNITED
AWARD CEREMONY

For upcoming titles please visit:

www.conniestokespublishing.co.uk